PRAISE FOR GOOD BOY

"It's Watership Down by George A. Romero."
Brian Keene - author of THE RISING

"Imagine the PLAGUE DOGS in a zombie apocalypse."
Garrett Cook - author of CRISIS BOY

"This is everything that's great about zombie fiction and animal protagonists."
Jay Wilburn - author of BEAUTIFUL DARKNESS

"Clark's narrative alternates between punching you in the gut and tugging at your heartstrings in this utterly unique apocalyptic tale. You need to read this book, now."
Pete Kahle, author of THE SPECIMEN

"Clark has redefined man's best friend."
Lucas Milliron – author of TIM E. LESS

"An amazing story ... With all the heart of The Incredible Journey, *but the teeth of* The Walking

Dead. Good Boy *is a real treat for horror fans!"*
Erin Kelly – author of the TAINTED MOONLIGHT
Series

"Clark's "Good Boy" brings back all of the memories
you have of your favorite animals...then kills them."
Jarod Barbee, DEATH'S HEAD PRESS

"A really fine piece of writing. It pulled me right
along and brought tears to my eyes at the end."
Mike Duke – author of LOW & CRAWL

"I cried ... And already miss him."
Erin Sweet Al-Mehairi - author of BREATHE,
BREATHE

ALSO BY THE AUTHOR:

BELLA'S BOYS
THE DEATH LIST
THE GOD PROVIDES
SUMMERHOME
A PRAYER FROM THE DEAD
IMMORAL DILEMMAS

COMING SOON:

THE WITCH OF NOVEMBER
WE ARE 13
THE TELLING OF THE BEES
WHIRLWIND

Good Boy

A Story of Extreme Survival Horror

A Novella By

Thomas R Clark

Nightswan Press
Syracuse
- 2024 -

GOOD BOY
A TALE OF SURVIVAL HORROR

Good Boy

TABLE OF CONTENTS

FOREWORD

I've done a foreword for Tommy before, but this one is special.

It's special because this story is not only my introduction to the beginning of Tommy's career, but it is also an introduction to Tommy, my friend.

Scares That Care in Virginia has a special place in people's hearts for so many reasons. The convention led people to a new kind of gathering where, no matter who you were, you were on the same level as everyone else who was there.

Celebrities, staff, vendors, readers—it didn't matter. We were all treated with respect, love, and kindness. I say all this because it meant everyone could hang out, chat about things we love, and network with people you might never get an opportunity to otherwise.

It so happened that in 2018, I attended for the first time with an entourage of Stitched Smile authors and staff. It was hectic, it was exciting, and it was new. For two years, I called them my staff and forged friendships with them.

I don't know about you, but I don't make friends easily.

At one point during the weekend, Tommy walked up to me and handed me a book. It was small and had this amazing little cover with a terrier. I looked closer and saw that the terrier, at first glance, looked to be happily trotting along but was actually carrying a rabid little animal in its mouth.

The hell?

Have you ever seen the Watership Down cover from 1972 with the rabbit and the compass? That's exactly what this was, but it had a dog with a rabid, bleeding animal in its mouth.

Now, let me take a minute here and let you in on a little secret.

Tommy is a smart fucking guy. And he's as sensitive as he is smart. But don't mistake that for weakness. He's definitely not a pussy. If you mess with anyone Tommy loves, he will rip your throat out and happily trot off with your bleeding carcass like this pooch on the cover. My point is: Tommy has a lot of marketing prowess.

Is he opinionated? Yep. Is he as blunt as a rolled-up doob? Fuck yes. But there is method to his madness, and you'll never doubt his passion.

Now, let me get back to this story. This little book, with barely over 100 pages in it, starts out, "I bite, I shake, I pull and I tear. It's how I fight, and today it's how I die."

I read that opening and put the book down for a

couple of days. I had to mentally prepare myself. We all love our pets. If you're a dog lover, you know our dogs will die to protect us. They will endure excruciating pain to champion us and whomever they consider to be part of their pack.

I, for one, would throw a human in the line of fire to save my dog. No qualms about it, either. I tell you that with no shame.

If you ask me one thing about Tommy that you should know, it's that he is as faithful and loyal to his friends as this book is about a fearless Jack Russell Terrier called Good Boy.

This was his debut novella, which he put in my hand personally. His baby. I held it for a long time, thinking about it, pondering the implications, my role in this unveiling, and the responsibility of it.

This story is brilliant, I thought to myself. No one wanted this moment more than Tommy did, and he chose me. There was no way I could say no to him. I just had to figure out how to say, "Yes."

And ever since then, Tommy has become a part of my pack.

So, read this story with the respect it deserves. He's earned it. He's grown into the fantastic writer and storyteller you all know him as right now. I'm honored to have been a part of that journey. Now, I'm putting this story in your hands.

"I bite, I shake, I pull and I tear. It's how I fight,

and today it's how I die," invokes fear, sadness, anger, maybe pride? It tells you the entire story in the first two sentences and compels you to read every word knowing it's going to end horribly.

And then what does he do . . .?

. . . Read the fuckin' book and find out.

- Lisa Vazquez

I bite, I shake, I pull, and I tear.
It's how I fight, and today it's how I die.

- Canid fight mantra

A *setting sun covers the land in a crimson blanket of waning light. Shadows cast long, dark streaks in the wake of twilight. One shadow stretches from a weathered, leafless tree. It is twisted and bent in unnatural manners. A tattered sheet of newspaper hangs from an errant tree limb. Wind blows, fluttering the parchment. A foreboding headline stands out in bold letters:*

BRAIN WORM PLAGUE

More words, smaller in print, follow …

Was it freed from its ancient, dormant state after the discovery of the virus in Antarctica? Did scientists bring it back from the International Space Station? Or is it a natural mutation? No one knows the cause behind the strain of rabies responsible for the roundworm mutation. The pandemic has spread across much of the country, and throughout the world, since the first reports of the infection came about earlier this year. With no known cure, infection from the mutated roundworms is a certain death sentence.

When asked about what is now being called "brain worms," Upstate Medical Contagious Disease expert Dr. Joan Rollins told the Post Standard, "It doesn't exactly attack the brain, so I don't know why it's being called brain worms. The worms attack the host nervous system, not the brain. They attach to the nerves, with the final result having much the same effect as a chemical nerve agent would in humans and mammals with a higher degree of cognitive ability. Smaller, less developed animals become vector carriers of the virus."

The Centers for Disease Control estimates the casualties from the brain worm infection to be in the millions before the end of summer. The virus can be easily passed by saliva from an infected animal. Infected humans lose control of motor functions and die a slow, painful death. CDC officials are working around the clock to isolate a vaccine for the killer virus.

The Governor has issued a state of emergency throughout the state of New York. If you or a loved one become infected, you are advised to remain in your home, it's your most comfortable form of hospice, as there is no cure for the infection. Any infected persons found traveling will be handled with extreme prejudice by authorities.

•

Under the shadow of these words, a pack of small dogs digs and roots through a small garden of rotting vegetables. Squashes and berries are plentiful, in all stages of ripening. They haven't eaten in a number of days, and their hunger obfuscates the danger skittering along the skeletal branches of the trees.

•

The squirrels appeared from nowhere, swarming as we foraged through the garbage pile. The rumbling in our bellies blinded us to the danger and made us careless. As a result, the infected critters took the smallest of us before we noticed their fetid stench. The offal smelled of spoiled cabbage, rot, and mildew. It was quite effective at masking their subtle, poisoned malodor. Within moments the squirrels were a black cloud, jumping from the branches of the trees, blotting out the setting sun.

Red-eyed and frothing at the mouth with a newfound taste for flesh, we watched the horde of rodents pursue us as we bolted back to the safety of our den. Under the trees and brush we ran, all while squirrels fell from the sky, a furry storm of impending doom. Driven mad, poisoned by the brain worms, they are many, but we are swift. Outrunning the infected was easy, but we knew this wasn't over, we knew they'd follow. They always did, the hunger of the brain worms saw to it.

It's been a winter since the brain worms came. We learned early on the parasite killed humans and many larger mammals. Reptiles, fish, and birds were immune, some other animals, too. The brain worms had a different effect on the smaller wild mammals. Squirrels and most of the varmints above ground were driven mad as the worms ate into their brains. The days of barking up trees at the bushy-tailed, nut hoarding rodents quickly became a thing of the past. Whereas barking once sent the squirrels racing away in fear of their lives, it now attracted insatiable hordes of pestilent beasts.

The infection took over their small bodies, animating them to serve the parasite's desire to feed and spread. Mindless, senseless killing ensued, or, even worse, maiming and infecting the wounded, turning them mad as the worms squirmed into their heads. We were safe from the infection. Long before anyone dreamed this would or could happen, our humans took us to see the *vet*, to protect against the thirst madness, with the *shots*.

I feel a brief moment of relief when we arrive at our burrow, the place we call our home since the plague struck, but it's fleeting. There is little time to warn the others and prepare a defense. The den is a series of expanded groundhog tunnels under the wood of a collapsed shed. Small animal skeletons are littered about, reminding us of our previous encounters with the infected. They've failed to penetrate our defenses in each previous attempt, and this should be no different. We dig in, splitting up to guard the entrances.

As predicted, the little monsters followed. Razor-sharp claws propel their black and gray bodies from the surrounding trees. The cloud pours down the tunnels to our subterranean home. The stench of the worms is our cue to stand firm.

Now we, the pack, *fight* them back as one. *We bite, we shake, we pull, we tear, and we kill.* Squirrel after squirrel dies, their backs or necks snapped by the power of our jaws and the fury of our desire to survive. On an individual basis, a poisoned squirrel is no problem. A quick snap of your jaws can break its neck, sending the brain worms into the dirt to search for a new host. When they become legion, they become a different issue altogether. You can't fight more than a few at once; if you're a dog you only own one set of jaws. In the tunnels we even the odds by dividing them.

Fighting them outside, in the open, is suicide. If you're not careful, the hordes of infected can surround you, cutting off all your possible escape routes. When you are vastly outnumbered, with nowhere to run for sanctuary, death or infection are inevitable. Once in the tunnels, we can even the odds. In the safety of the narrow passageways, only a few can enter at a time without clogging the way with critter bodies.

The burrow is black as night. Long ago we learned the affliction dulled their senses, their sight is weak in the dark. The stench of the worms overpowers their sense of smell here. This makes them blind on most accounts and gives us even further advantage. It's why we've been able to live as long as we have, hidden under a world in chaos. Still, wave after wave of rodents come with gnashing teeth and scratching claws.

We can't see a damn thing under the surface, but we can smell the bastards. We fight them back, and risk poisoning ourselves on their putrid blood. It must be done for the survival of the pack; some of us must make a sacrifice. The numbers of us who were given *shots* are dwindling and whatever protection it offered is fading. For the pack's survival, I bite, I shake, I pull, and I tear for as long as I can.

A squirrel slips by me as I snap his friend's neck with one twist of my jaws. I drop the body and cry for help, hoping the pack hears me. We can't let the freaks into the burrow. Allowing even a single infected to break our ranks means failure. I turn and strike, catching it by the tail, pulling the foul creature back. It fights harder, the creature's paws catching each and every crevasse in the red clay and dirt wall, leaving furrows as it tries with all its might to escape my hold.

The rabbit living with us, my mate's friend and companion, comes to my aid after hearing my bark. You may think a prey animal like a bunny would be a coward in a fight, hiding in fear for his life. Not our bunny. He's as tall as my mate and just as big around, with a temper to match his girth.

He honks in defiance at the squirrel and thumps it in the side with his powerful rear legs, crushing the intruder's ribs, an audible crunch is my cue to act. I catch the beast's tail and jerk my head back. The squirrel's paw is snagged on an exposed root. The force of my tug is so great, I rip the arm out at the shoulder. Blood flies, splattering the rabbit with gore. He honks, again, this time to express his displeasure.

I can't see it, but I can smell the aroma of blood. It sends me into a frenzy, and I dive at the onslaught. I'm not alone. There is a fury of teeth, claws, bone, and ripped flesh as the cat, another of our pack, joins me. Hissing and growling, she doesn't play with her prey. Unlike the rest of us, kitty can see in the dark. She slashes and kills, without prejudice, anything with red eyes and a bushy tail ends up in pieces. Bits of squirrel ricochet off the walls of the burrow. We've sprayed and marked the den, making the earth itself poisonous to the brain worms escaping the mutilated bodies. They sizzle as they land.

The worms controlling another squirrel give it the balls to think it can get past me. I catch its head in my mouth and slam my jaws shut. The creature's skull shatters. It tastes of worms, brain, and another flavor I don't recognize. I spit out the remains, the ammonia smell of my saliva killing the worms permeates my nose and drives me into a sneezing fit. The dead squirrel's body lay prone in the dirt. I mount it at the shoulders and hump its headless corpse, a victory dance of our dominance over the infected.

Then it's over. The invasion stops, or at least the assault does. It becomes quiet except for the dripping of blood and viscera. This has happened before. The squirrels plugged the entrance to our burrow. This means there are more of the little bastards, bottle-necked at the top, chewing their way through their brethren. It has bought us some time to rest.

We regroup in the common chamber, sniffing each other for wounds and brain worms like we would for ticks. There are none.

This time.

I'm anxious, pacing in circles. If and when the infected dig through, I will continue to *fight*. The pack will *fight* with me, because I am the *leader*, and I am the leader because I have a *name*.

A *name* is something to be proud of. Mine hangs from my neck, a piece of metal with scratches and paint, and though I can't read it, I know what it says. It is my *name* and *names* make us who we are. With their words and language, only humans can bestow a *name* upon us, and there are no more humans left to do so, at least none I've seen since the plague struck. I fear for the puppies growing inside my mate, they will not have *names*. Without a *name*, they will become much like the woodchuck and his family we now live with. Backwoods and uneducated. They won't know how to *sit*, *stay*, or *look*, which are the essentials to staying alive, therefore life will be hard on them.

It's a shame none of these pups will ever know a human. Though many humans were unpredictable and to be avoided, the humans I experienced were benevolent. My humans gave me my *name*, they gave my mate a *name*. They gave the rabbit a *name*, though he doesn't remember it. Rabbits can be that way, forgetful. I call him what he is. He's a rabbit, he's our *bunny*. The cat, she has a *name* too, though she refuses to acknowledge it. Cat's are always that way, stubborn and arrogant, thinking they know it all. Because of this, it's easier to call her what she is, she's our *kitty-cat*.

The cat and rabbit have been with us since the brain worms came. The bunny forages in the grasses near our den under the cover of darkness. The cat comes and goes as she pleases, hunting at night, bringing back fresh kills of bird or fish for all of us to eat. But never rabbit. It would be rude to our buck-toothed friend, not to mention many wild rabbits are infected. Better safe than sorry.

We are a feisty, diverse lot, our pack. We are small in stature but bold in stance, and these traits have helped us survive. We are brave, tenacious, and loyal to one another in our pack, be they dog, cat, woodchuck, or rabbit. For all we know, we're the only ones left, besides the infected and the birds feeding off the dead.

My mate and I are working terriers, puddin' dogs, as are the others in the pack, though none of them have pedigrees or *papers* like my mate and I did, when humans made things of this nature important.

My coat is white and wire haired, with a brown spot on my ear. My mate's shorter than me and smooth coated, black and white with a brown head. Furthering how special my mate and I are, our tails are docked, and we don't possess dew claws. The others, by contrast, are a mixed lot without the special treatment of a dog with *papers*.

Not that *papers* mattered anymore. My mate took it a step further, she was once a *show* dog, pampered and groomed. She is like the rest of the pack—a survivor, pregnant, living in dirt, eating moldy cabbage and rotten fish. We're all equal, and in this new world, you're either dead, alive, or infected.

Now I must decide. Is it wise to stay here any longer? This isn't the first time the squirrels, or another infected beast, followed one of us home. The snow is gone, the flowers are blooming, and the trees are leafy. The puppies will be born soon. The dead squirrels will smell of rot and make disease, disease our *shots* won't protect us from. These thoughts hang heavy in my mind as I limp to the center of the burrow, where my pregnant mate rests in a bed of grasses, waiting to give birth to our puppies. The cat and the rabbit sit at her sides, keeping her safe and warm. The cat's purring relaxes us all. I smell and hear the pack arriving at the center of the burrow with us. I smell worry and fear among them. They share in my concerns. The others whine and whimper. I'm afraid, too, but I am the *leader*, and they look up to me. I can't show fear. I must show strength. For my pack, for my mate, and for my unborn puppies.

I miss the comforts of living with humans. I miss nesting in the blankets on their bed. I miss playing with the *toys* and *cookies*, too. Most of all, I miss hearing my *name*. I don't miss the *bath* much, but I suppose I could use one right about now. We've not seen a human since we escaped into the wild. Their lights and fires went out after the houses burned and the machines stopped running, after the brain worms got into all the wild animals' heads and killed anything in their path.

I find my *ball*. Other than my *name* hanging from my neck, it is the last remnant of my life with humans. I find comfort in it, and chewing it keeps my jaws strong for the *fight*. But it also relaxes me and helps me think. I pick it up and lay next to my mate. I close my eyes and think of what to do. Rest will help me decide.

•

The little white dog lays on the ground, curled into a ball of fur. He is safe in a groundhog burrow, deep under the earth. His eyes flutter to a close as he drifts off to sleep. It's a restless sleep brought on by the adrenaline still coursing through his bloodstream. His eyes dart to and fro as his mind processes the day's events through the magic of dreams. He kicks a leg and whimpers, the sigh catching the attention of the cat he calls a friend. The feline moves closer to her canine companion, kneading the earth with her front paws before settling. She begins to purr. Her touch calms the dog, and he settles into a deep sleep, remembering ...

•

I think back to when the infected came, not long ago, before the last snow fell. My quick thinking saved us at first, finding the woodchuck burrow and negotiating with the inhabitants for shelter, promising protection in return for safety. If not for the mild winter, it's possible we would've died. Another trick of the tail working in our favor, no different than discovering the woodchuck burrow, I guess. It wouldn't be the end of the world if living were easy. Not like it used to be before the brain worms.

Our humans loved us. We lived with the cat and the rabbit, an unorthodox living arrangement in the wild, without a doubt. But here, the balance of home

The infected animal erupted out of the hedge.

made it feel right. The family of humans, the *Daddy* and the *Momma* and their *Boy* held us in high regard. My mate befriended the bunny and the cat, and I followed suit. It wasn't by choice, bunny tastes good and cats, well, they're assholes. As long as I can remember, I've always been a *Good Boy*, doing the right thing. Pleasing my humans and my mate made me happy; it gave me purpose. So I made friends with bunny and the cat.

Bunny is a salty old bag of ears, and I often found it easy to manipulate him, making him thump and honk, playing off his fears of being eaten. It's ironic how this skill has helped me keep him alive since the plague struck. His human *Boy* caught the brain worms first. He came home early from school, ill, reeking of rot. It's a stench we all now know is the worms shitting as they eat into the brains of their victims. It makes a skunk smell like gourmet snacks. By nightfall, the *Daddy* and *Momma* left to drive the *Boy* to the doctor, but they came back before long, frantic and scared. Sirens blared throughout the night and flashing lights flew by at an alarming rate. It hurt my ears, and I barked until my voice was raw. A disaster of some manner was unfolding in the outside world, keeping them, all of us, here. The *Boy* died by morning, the worms slithering in and out of any orifice in the cranial area.

Kitty, however, is another story. Always the

Momma's favorite, and not afraid to let you know. She gives fewer craps than a badger about anything but herself, but she stays with us. The *Momma* came next, becoming infected because of coddling her dying child. The *Daddy* wanted to help her, but she wouldn't let him, locking herself in a room with the cat. She was afraid of infecting the *Daddy*. The *Momma* wondered aloud why none of the animals got sick, not one. How would they know our *shots* from the *vet* protected us from the infection?

She asked the cat to protect my mate, and the cat vowed to stay by her side. The *Momma* opened the door and let the cat out and closed it before the *Daddy* could stop her. First I heard the lock turn. Then I heard the gunshot. I smelled sulfur and blood, burnt flesh, and dead brains. The blood leaked under the door, pooling as it coagulated, the brain worms twisting and writhing in the puddle as they died. The *Daddy* screamed.

"*No!*" He pounded the door with his fists, and crumpled into a heap, on his knees, his fists slamming into the wood. I don't like the word *No*; it always leads to something bad. The *Daddy* never tried to open the door back up afterward. The cat led me away, to my mate. There was nothing more to see.

The *Daddy* kept us all in the living room after this. He held a gun, and smelled of fear. I tried to tell him the brain worms he feared, there were none in the house, living at least. Instead of calming down, he let me go out to *potty*. I didn't need to *potty*, but he let me out and I couldn't count on when he would again, so I took advantage of it.

Outside, the world felt different, it smelled different. Something in the air stunk of the brain worms. The *Daddy* stood on the porch, his gun in hand, scanning the street as I sniffed for a spot to piss. I didn't see the mangy, infected fox until it struck.

Neither did the *Daddy*.

The diseased creature sprung at him from the bushes, biting into the *Daddy*'s neck and locking down its jaws. Mangey and hairless, it no longer resembled a fox, instead the infection made it frightening to behold. Screaming in agony, the *Daddy* ripped the creature off him. Blood spouted from the open wound. The fox bounced off the deck and crashed into the flower pots, shrieking and squealing, its teeth snapping and feet flailing. Centrifugal force carried it through the pots, smashing the porcelain and clay, and off the deck into the hedge. The *Daddy* threw his hand over his gaping wound, hoping to stop the bleeding, but with little success. The fluid continued to spit through his fingers, making crimson splatters on the deck. The infected animal erupted out of the hedge, poised to strike the *Daddy* again.

This time it met me.

I struck it in midair, my jaws catching the beast

at the back of its neck. We rolled on the ground. I refused to release my grip. I found my feet and raised my haunches, keeping my head and, in turn, its neck in the dirt. I *shook*! I *pulled*! The worms tickled at my lips, but sizzled and shrunk in a smoky haze when my saliva touched them. I pulled, tore, and ripped the fox's head off. Blood, or at least what should be blood but wasn't anymore, spurted out of the gaping wound, covering the deck in a slick, black goo. The head bounced off the door and rolled into a corner. The former home of the fox's head was now a stump, teeming with the little worms. After a moment, the body stopped kicking, but the head still thrashed at nothing. The jaws continued to snap at nothing for a few more moments, then without blood, or worms, to keep it alive, the head joined the rest of its body and died. The worms controlling its motor functions squirmed about from the head and body, seeking a new host but none were to be found. They dropped into the dust and leaves, shriveled and died.

The loud retort of a firearm, followed by the crashing of glass and metal, scared me. I looked up to see the *Daddy* laying on the floorboards. He fired the rifle into the roof of the porch as a reflex. He landed on the porch, writhing in pain as the blood spurted from his neck, his body jamming the door open. I ran to his aid, but it was too late. The stink of the brain worms lingered about him. I saw them wiggling around the wound on his neck, splitting, multiplying, and spreading at an alarming speed. In no time they squirmed out from the blood and torn flesh, crawling up his face into his ears, eyes, mouth, and up his nose. I can't help him. My mate and the cat joined me at his side, but there was nothing any of us could do. The *Daddy* bled to a merciful death before the brain worms could drive him mad.

Knowing we couldn't stay in the human home, the four of us left, not sure where we would end up. The dangers in the outside world were too much to fathom. With the exception of kitty, prior to this, our exposure to the outside world was controlled by the *Daddy* and *Momma*. This was limited to car rides ending at parks, pet stores, family friends, or the *vet*.

The landscape changed, much to my surprise. By night, human buildings burned bright in the dark of night, not with their typical lights, but with fire. Chaos ran rampant under the glowing full moon. What the brain worms didn't kill, the mob devoured. Humans killed humans out of fear of infection.

During the day, the birds circled overhead, waiting to feast on the remains of the recently dead, or fresh meat. Our mismatched pack fell under the latter category. Birds were not our friends.

The survival learning curve for our fellowship often worked in our favor, as we learned about our own immunities to the brain worm infection. Much of it occurred by accident, in particular the effect of our saliva or urine, how it melted the worms into harmless puddles of goo. Staying alive dictated we travel at night and hide during the day to avoid the infected. Even then, it was best to stay in wooded land and fields, giving us cover. Birds were a constant threat, and the cover of brush kept them at bay. This caution led us to finding the other dogs who now make up our pack.

We discovered them trapped within an elaborate series of outside kennels. They broke free of their cages, but the surrounding fence trapped them. For whatever reason, they hadn't touched it. The stench of dog dirt permeated the air about the stockade and was a beacon, leading us to them. Before the plague, this was a place where puppies were bred to be sold. Both my mate and I came from breeders, but those humans treated us with love. It was obvious the humans here cared about one thing: selling puppies.

The trapped puppies grew into adults, but wild, without training or guidance. The building once housing their humans burned to the ground at some point. They were low on food, and water was available through muddy puddles in the compound. This made them desperate to be free. Dead and rotting bodies of infected varmints littered the kennel grounds, all dispatched by the trapped pack. Still I wondered, why hadn't they broken free or dug out. And then I saw it. They believed the fence was still alive and ready to fry whomever touched it.

Chicken wire attached to tall posts and fear of the once electrified fencing kept them imprisoned. This was when I figured out they weren't very bright. Without humans, there was no electricity. They could have broken free at any time, but the fear they learned of the fence's potential to shock stayed with them. They barked at my mate and I as we approached them. I snapped back and tugged on the fencing. The pack shirked in fear, expecting to watch my hair stand on end and smoke to pour from my nostrils. Instead the fence came apart.

As one would expect, their excitement at being freed was repaid with their devotion. Now they strive on, with one focus in life: serve me. As far as making decisions on their own went, the others were helpless, which explained their inability to escape the kennels. However, they took orders without question and executed them with blind passion.

We were scavenging for food when we stumbled upon the woodchucks. I was even more surprised to find a varmint, let alone a family of them, not infected with the brain worms. They were terrified of us, and ran off with their little chucklings to their burrow before we could explain ourselves. It wasn't hard to track them, the uninfected left a distinct scent behind. It smelled clean, as did the trail leading to their den. Their burrow was hidden under a rickety shed near a series of burned-out human homes. It was a perfect hiding place for the coming winter, which the groundhogs assured us would be mild. When it became clear there was no interest in eating any marmot, they allowed us to move into the burrow, but on the condition it would be for the winter season. Constantly insisting this would be a temporary thing, our uneasy alliance with the groundhogs began. And now, as my consciousness returns, I fear our cohabitation will be coming to an end.

•

The little dog stirs awake, his feline companion still snuggled at his side. He kicks in place as the memories linger in his mind. Something soothes him, the soft purring of the cat, and he sighs. The speech of animals, if you would call it speech, is a combination of body language and vocalizations. And though it is not spoken in the same manner as, say a human would communicate, it is a universal tongue acknowledged by all beasts. Even the least empathetic of humans will recognize when a domesticated animal is attempting to "tell them something."

•

I wake up, kicking in place as the memories linger. Kitty-cat is there, laying next to me, purring, and it's calming. I ask her if it is time to go, and she agrees it may be. Quite often it has been the cat who has advised me on how to proceed. I can't say she has ever steered us wrong. She may be an asshole, but she keeps her word. Regardless, I still don't trust her. After all, she is a cat.

She speaks up, stalks about, rubs her shoulder against my chin and says she found a place, a human place, still standing. It's clean, warm, and safe, and she found a hidden way inside. She has seen lights there at night and thinks humans might be there, but she's never seen one when she's been inside. She says it's not far from the burrow, and she can guide us there tonight—when the squirrels and hawks can't see us in the dark. I question this. Why haven't we found this human house before? She tells me it's on the far side of the *highway*, on the other side of a sea of grass.

I stop in my tracks, terrified. The *highway*? This scares me almost as much as the squirrels. We're, rather I'm, not supposed to go near the *highway*. But to reach this house, we'd be crossing the *highway*, a death zone for animals. I've never dared venture across the *highway*, or even back within sight of it, knowing full well what it could do to any of us. The human cars moving faster than we can run, with disastrous results for any critter crossing its black lanes. The dead deer thing, its rotten, decaying smell returns to my mind with the visual cue. I sneeze, shaking my head to erase the vision from my mind.

The cat tells me to relax and stop acting like the rabbit, or the other dogs in the pack when we found them, scared of a dead electric fence. She says she crossed the *highway*; it wasn't dangerous anymore, ever since the brain worms killed all the people. She's not wrong. For much the same reason the others in our pack feared the fence, I feared the *highway*. It makes sense to me. With no humans, there would be no human machines to run us over and crush our bones. Regardless of these facts, my fearfulness of the *highway* isn't without merit. I earned it, as well as the *Daddy*'s wrath.

Once, long ago, I ran off, chasing a little bird. I got as far as the *highway*; I watched the birdie fly into the *highway*'s zone, then disappear in the chaos of racing machines. I discovered the crushed remains of what was a deer at one point, a grim guardian of the *highway* before me. It stank of death and decay, maggots squirming about the carcass. The skull of the dead animal welcomed me, beckoning me to pass, its toothy grimace formed by holes in the fetid, rotting flesh still clinging to its body. One eye was plucked clean out of its head, the other turned white and stared into my soul.

I froze in place and watched as the human machines roared down the road. I turned and ran home and received a stern scolding from the *Daddy*. I didn't care, I tucked my tail and took my lumps. Any punishment from the *Daddy* or *Momma* was better than the alternative the *highway* offered me. This would be the last time I ran off chasing a bird or any other animal. Now I weigh the options. Stay here and we die. Leave here and we risk death.

The *treat* at the end?

A human house. With blankets for the puppies. Maybe even water or food. I nudge my mate for her opinion. She thinks about it for a moment, considering the options, and agrees with the cat. It will be dangerous, moving all of us there, but it can be done. The other dogs agree. Not surprising is the rabbit. He balks at first, honking and thumping the earthen floor in fear, but rabbits are afraid of most anything innocuous, most of all change. With a little coaxing, he relents and decides to come with us. Our woodchuck hosts are not as accepting of the plan. They will stay with their chucklings, believing they were fine before they met us and will be fine after we're gone. I fear for them, but they care not. This is their home. They are happy their unwanted guests are leaving, hiding behind the illusion they would be safer without us bringing so much attention to the burrow. I think the cat made them more uncomfortable than the infected.

Regardless, the decision is made. As night has fallen, we will leave and find this human home.

I gather the pack, my mate, the rabbit, and the cat. I take my *ball*. We move out of the burrow in silence in the long tunnel, apart from the main entryways. I'm the last to go, after my mate, and watch as the woodchuck collapses the outlet behind us, barring a return. He's a fool. He's also blocked his escape. We crawl on to exit and see, far behind us in the moonlight, a shifting and breathing mound. It is a writhing mass of infected squirrels focused on digging through their brethren to devour the now trapped groundhogs. The mound shrinks in size, then more until it disappears. They broke through. We hear the sounds of crunching and the shrill screams of marmots. We cover the exit hole. I look to my mate, she sighs in relief, aware we could've been trapped in the burrow. We kick extra dirt onto the pile to be safe.

A full moon sets low, filling the skyline. Bright and orange, it peeks out from behind the distant hills. It illuminates the night, shining through the thin clouds, resembling long, gray fingers stretching across the horizon. Free of the ambient light of man, the stars of the galaxy shine bright in the sky. Mars, once known as the planet of war, is the brightest. She sits next to the lunar spectacle, a red twinkle staring back at the earth. A meteor shower streaks through the clouds, disappearing in the glow of the moon.

The burned out remains of homes litter the landscape; debris is spread about, filling the remains of a suburban development. The pack of small dogs, now joined by a cat and a rabbit, quietly move through the brush. In another age, it would be an odd fellowship to behold. In this new world born of a plague the living are aberrant, and nothing is out of the question. The animals sniff about, staying close to shrubs and trees, following the cat.

They pass a storefront, its windows smashed out; the shelves are empty. **WILLIAMS GROCERY** is written in bold letters across the store facade. By contrast, a blue and green newspaper rack is full of year-old newspapers. The display is still attached to rusting poles supporting an awning over the entrance, no one is alive to read the pages. The fellowship of animals weaves through the wreckage and

makes their way to the rear of the building. If they could read, they would have seen the same head-line emblazoned across the top of each newspaper:
IS THIS THE END?
The smaller words below ask more questions and give no answers.

"Is the Round Worm Plague the biblical pestilence heralding the end of times? Some would say the 'brain worms,' a result of a mutation in the rabies virus and common roundworms, is indeed an instrument of the divine. With no known cure, infection is a death sentence. The disease has been spread by vermin, typically rats and squirrels, infected by the virus.

"Multiple theories exist, surrounding the outbreak, which was only discovered earlier this year in the southwestern United States. In less than eight months, it spread throughout the world via rats and other vermin on cargo ships. It has brought the bulk of human civilization to its knees.

"Before being ushered off to the safety of his bunker, the president's final executive order, giving state governors the ability to declare martial law and curfew, has done nothing to quell the spreading of the disease. Most municipalities across New York and the nation are now closed. The stock market has been in a steady crash since closing a week ago ..."

But dogs can't read. If they could, they would educate the author if he was still alive. The dogs and cat knew, through experience, animals inoculated against the rabies virus were immune to the brain worms ...

•

At night, the world is full of light and shadow and not much in between. When humans ruled the world, it was different. Danger existed, but the dangers could be avoided if you would *sit*, *stay*, or *look*. These words didn't matter anymore. Now the buildings are empty, their lights no longer brightening the night. The cars, trucks, and flying machines lay silent and unmoving. The dangers are new.

We follow the cat and the rabbit, their sight and hearing is far more keen than ours, plus the cat knows where we are going. The rest of us keep our ears high, we sniff and are wary of scents foul or wrong. We move as a single unit, close together, making sure none fall behind. This slows us down. My mate is having difficulty with this trip; her belly is full with puppies and ready to burst. I ask the cat how much farther we need to go; she tells me it isn't far. I find it hard to believe her; we've not even made it to the *highway*. The human's buildings we've run past so far are all burned out, stinking of charcoal, mildew, and rot. None of them are a safe place for puppies to be born.

The houses become fewer, replaced by the remnants of larger buildings set inside vast lots of the black ground used to make *highways*. There are more instances where we are exposed, where we can be seen. I don't like this, and with my mate's condition, I like it even less. Our goal isn't to attract attention; it's to find a new home where the puppies can be born in safety. Since we left the woodchuck burrow, I've watched the moon move higher in the sky.

We come to a bridge and follow the small stream of stagnant water setting under it, avoiding the *road* above it as much as possible. I'd rather we not take our chances with what we may encounter out in the open. Though not as dangerous as the *highway*, a *road* is still a threat. Below the bridge isn't much safer. The infected hide in places like this at night. We are lucky none are to be found. The brackish water reeks of waste and sewage. Bunny hates it, the toxic mud gets on his fur, as much as it sticks between our toes. It stinks. I reach the exit and scratch my paws into the dry dirt and grasses leading up the shallow bank and the black ground, trying to remove the mud. It doesn't work very well. All I can smell, all any of us can smell, is the mud. Kitty wrinkles her nose and bounds into the black lot.

She stops and looks back to us. We all stop, *sit, stay,* and *look*. Kitty-cat insists we follow. The pack *looks* to me for assurance. I think for a moment, then with reluctance, I give in and follow her. I know we have no choice but to stay the course.

We move together, our nails clicking on the black ground. It sounds like rain, and echoes against the walls of the structure still standing before us.

The building was once a place where humans stored food. Now its windows are gone, and the shelves are bare. The roof extends over the lot, offering us shelter from above. You never know what will be flying about at night, looking for food. We avoid the broken glass littering the black ground, fully aware it could cut our paws. Kitty keeps a constant pace just ahead of us, weaving between the poles supporting the roof. It looks like things will go smooth, until she reaches a tall metal box attached to one of the poles, and stops.

Kitty raises her hackles, her hair sticking straight up. She hisses and retreats from the box, stepping backward one foot at a time. I stop in my tracks and prepare to strike at anything. The others follow, but not before maneuvering around my mate, protecting her. A chorus of low growls warning of our strength. The rabbit thumps and honks to insure anyone who doesn't get it, does. Bunny can be a brave soul, with a pack of dogs surrounding him.

Kitty-cat gets a safe distance from the box and stops. I run to her side. She can smell and hear something infected in the box. My nose is dulled by the mud, blinded to what the cat indicates. She stands with her haunches raised, ready to pounce and strike at anything stepping out of the box. I stand alert, ready to *fight*, watching the kitty for any cues she may give. The box rattles and shakes, but nothing steps out from inside it. Nothing visible, at least. A light breeze blows down the causeway, and we all discover why the kitty was on her guard.

There are a few things in the world you will never forget the smell of. The good things come to mind first. Your human master, a summer day, a tasty meal. Then there are the bad things like spoiled meat, brain worms ... and skunks. The latter is almost, but not quite as terminal as brain worms. Skunk stink fuses with you, it becomes part of you. It's a vile, sulfuric, malodor to be avoided at all costs. It hovered around the metal box, an invisible barrier barring any safe passage to anyone foolish enough to walk past its epicenter.

Kitty's growl grew as loud as mine when we saw something fall out of the back side of the box. It landed on the black ground with a wet plop. This was followed by another sick, dripping sound, and then another. The rest of the pack continue to huddle behind kitty and I, encircling my mate with the bunny at her side. The cat jumps and pounces at something near us.

Her claws grasp on to something I can't see in the dark. But I can smell it, as much as I can smell the skunk stench. It's unmistakable and wretched: brain worms. But where are the infected? The others

The skunk takes a few more listing steps...

detect it, as well, wrinkling their noses and shrinking back, tightening their circle around my mate and the bunny.

Kitty swats something into the air. It flies before me, making a wet slapping sound as it bounces off the ground into the wall of the building. It's small—the size of a chipmunk but the wrong colors—and covered in a fine coat of striped fur, with four legs and a tail. Brain worms squirm from about the thing's mouth and eyes. It struggles to its feet, the brain worms urging it on. I don't wait for it to find any prey and jump on it, holding the small body down with one paw as I rip the head off. It tastes rancid. I gag and spit it out, my jowls numb as my immunities work against the infection. Steam rises from my mouth as errant worms dissolve in my saliva.

The cat isn't idle. She swipes and bites at the other things as they mill around the metal box. Kitty meows loudly, catching my attention. I turn my head to see something striped and hairy has fallen out of the box and landed on top of her.

The cat jumps back to a safe distance away from it. At first it reminds me of a badger, then I realize, it is indeed a skunk. It hisses and claws at the cat. Kitty stands her ground between us and the skunk. It doesn't seem to be infected, there are no brain worms snaking around the animal's snout, ears, and eyes. The skunk twists around and raises its tail high in the air, ready to spray its noxious scent glands.

Nothing happens. Instead we are greeted with a horrific sight.

Projecting out from the skunk's posterior is a pair of brain worm infested heads and the upper torsos of a pair of the things. And I figure out what it was I just killed, a skunk kit. The front paws of each of the infected kits are pushing and clawing their way out of their mother's sack. They break free and fall on the ground at her feet. The skunk's back side is a gaping hole, dripping mucus and goo.

I wonder, how is it the kits are infected but the mother isn't? The dire reality of our situation sets in. I look at my mate. She's still in the safeguard of our pack. But that won't save our unborn puppies from the brain worms. Without a human *vet* to give the *shots*, it doesn't matter if they have *names* or not. I hope they have some immunity, carried on from their mother, but I'm not confident in this. The odds are in favor of our puppies ending up like the skunk's litter of kits, carriers of the brain worms.

Kitty-cat's growl alerts me to her plan, and she pounces on the back of the skunk, digging her claws into the animal's sides and biting her teeth deep into its neck. The skunk shakes and rolls, knocking kitty off. I stand firm between the box and the pack, the first line of defense if the skunk breaks free of the cat.

Kitty is a killing machine. She's built to be the

life of the party on occasions such as this. Cats, as a rule, were born to be the ultimate carnivorous predator. Nature outfitted her for the affair with long, retractable claws, and an innate sense of balance, suited well for both terrestrial and arboreal tasks. Her eyes allow her to see in almost complete darkness.

She uses these skills and abilities to herd the skunk, batting at it, taunting it, forcing it to move away from our path.

The skunk, on the other paw, can't see anything further than she can spit. Unable to secrete its noxious gas, she has no choice but to comply to the cat's wishes. Skittering back and through the remains of her offspring, she's also on the verge of being infected by the same brain worms once eating through her kits.

The cat is too busy forcing the skunk into capitulation to notice what's going on behind her prey. I watch as brain worms evacuate the dead bodies of the skunk kits. They slither up the mother skunk's legs and enter the gaping wound on her behind. The animal twitches and shakes as the writhing worms burrow into her flesh. The skunk takes a few more listing steps, and she stops moving. She teeters for a moment, and drops to the black ground in a clump.

Kitty-cat and I watch and wait. We know what will come next. The brain worms were burrowing through the skunk's body, working their way to the brain.

When they arrived, the worms would take control of the skunk's motor functions, turning it into a vessel of death. The tension and anticipation builds as the moments pass, but the skunk doesn't move.

In the far distance we all hear the distinct retort of a human gun. On cue all of us—every dog, cat, and rabbit—turn our heads away from the skunk, to the direction the crack resonated from. The echo of the shot, bouncing through the empty and ramshackle structures fades to nothing. Everything is silent, we all remain still. Then I remember the infected mother skunk and turn my attention back to it.

The skunk vanished.

Where could it have gone? I nudge kitty-cat and charge forward. She's as mystified as me over the disappearing skunk. We run behind the building. The moonlight shines bright in the back lot. There's nothing but the path to the *highway.*

•

We walk past the large building, careful to look for other infected creatures, and discover the *highway* hidden behind it. There are vehicles, as I feared, but none are moving, much to my relief. The moonlight reflects off the myriad of windshields, and though the air is thick with the smell of metal and fuel, I can see they are all abandoned. A tall chain-link fence bars our way, causing us to stop. The cat shows us where a tree has fallen on the fence, bringing it down, allowing us passage to the other side and the road.

Though there is no movement, we still *stay*. I *sit*, I *look* both ways. The *highway* is always deceiving. You never know if one of the machines will strike out of nowhere, turning you into a messy pile of crushed bones and flesh. We wait until we are sure. After some time placating my fear of the road, the cat nudges me. She reminds me, there are no humans left. She accomplishes this in her own unflattering manner, sticking her rear in my face. She runs across the lanes all the way to the other side. I hear her growl in impatience. *No humans. No machines,* I remind myself.

"*No highway!*" The *Daddy* shouts in my memory.

I sneeze and give the command to *go*. The rest of the pack run as one unit, across one lane, over the median to the next lane. I *stay* until all the others cross. Everyone makes it over, to my relief. We go down into a gully on the other side. It leads to a stream and another metal, chain-link fence, stopping our progress. The rabbit thumps, agitated we've run into another obstacle. I look to the clever kitty-cat, for guidance. She's taken this path before and shows us where the links come apart from a post. The gap is large enough for us to slink through. The cat goes first, then the rabbit and the other dogs in our pack. After my mate is through and safe on the other side with her cargo intact, I go.

And I get snagged on a link of the fence by my collar.

I can't move. I drop my *ball* and let loose a frightened whine. The others know something is wrong, they hear the duress in my tone. They grow more panicked by my cries. My mate tries to pull on the fence, but it doesn't help. I stop crying to focus on escaping. I try to work with her, but it makes it worse. I feel the link hooking deeper onto my collar as it rubs against my neck.

The cat interjects and unfurls her claws to cut the collar, but I will not let her. It holds my *name*, and without my *name*, I am nothing. I tug and pull as hard as I can, but I'm still stuck. The fence rattles, a symphony of metal clanging off metal, vibrating the links up and down its course. It's a dinner bell for the brain worm infected. Nervousness sets in as I struggle, but I will not sacrifice my collar or my *name*.

A high-pitched screech pierces my ears. The tone sounds warbled, out of tune. All of the dogs hear it. Their ears perk up straight, and they turn their heads to the sound. The cat and the rabbit, too. The rabbit honks, thumps and jumps under a log for safety. The cat senses the urgency. She uses her paws and tries to untangle the fence link from my collar. It doesn't work. The cat is irritated. She meows, the annoyance in her tone tells me the house she found is just over the hill, past this stream. I work harder to free myself, but it doesn't work. The screeching grows louder, closer.

An infected bat lands on the fence just above my head. The cat swats it away, her claws ripping its disfigured face off in the process. Another bat lands, then another, all infected with brain worms, all hungry for my flesh, any flesh. My mate cries in fear, terrified. The cat, her ears laid flat, pounces. She jumps to the top of the fence and catapults off, landing on all fours in the center of the fusion. Her hair is standing on end, her tail tucked low as she swipes her claws in a wild, wide arc, each blow striking and killing a bat. They keep coming, landing on both sides of the fence now. The other dogs get into the fray, biting and stomping on the infected bats. They're easier to kill than the squirrels, but they are many more than we can handle in the open.

Bats are landing all about me now. The cat is doing her best to keep them off me, but in doing so she's getting nipped in the behind. She flips on her back and catches a bat with her hind quarters and rips it in half. Blood and guts and brain worms spill out, covering both of us in gore. The force of her rolling frees my collar from the chain link, and I burst through to the other side. I grab my *ball* as the fence slaps closed, blocking any further use of the gateway. The cat turns onto her feet, assesses the situation, and jumps to the top of the fence. Before she can react, flying bats swarm her, knocking her back. She holds on to the post with one leg, sticking out from the infected animals latching on to her body. They stick to her, bat after bat until we can no longer see the cat. Her paw loses its grip, the weight of all those bats too much for a lone paw. I can hear her screaming in agony, albeit muffled by the bodies surrounding her.

It pains me. We cannot help her after all she did to help me get free; with the fence now sealed, we are locked out, trapped on the other side. The ball of bats covering the cat falls to the other side of the fence and rolls back down the gully. Those flying follow and soon there is a heap of brain worm-infected bats in the gully, eating through each other to get to what little is left of kitty by this point.

My mate howls in grief. The others in the pack join her in mourning our fallen friend. Bunny honks and thumps in unison. Chewing on my *ball*, I notice an errant bat fly over the fence and land in the stream. I bark to the others to stop. Our cries are attracting more bats. Mourning our friend could result in more dying.

I sneeze in frustration. Because of the infected, we don't have the luxury to grieve our fallen friend. We must move now while the infected bats are distracted. The rabbit doesn't argue about this one bit, and he is the first to jump across the small stream. The rest of us follow with haste. The stream's edge leads up an embankment and into a field of tall grass. In the distance I see it, we all see it. The human house, standing tall and untouched. Much to my surprise, there is a light shining from a window at the house's highest point. Our kitty-cat was speaking the truth. I look to my mate; her swollen belly is moving with the puppies she carries. She sees the building too and understands we will soon have shelter. Now, could humans be here? I yip, urging the rest of our pack to follow and carry on.

•

We move into the grass. Something about this place smells off, but not enough to deter us. It stinks of chemicals covered by sweet flowers. It isn't long before I run into a large, carved rock with human scratches on it. We find more rocks. It's obvious this place isn't an empty field; it has a purpose. The grasses start to recede in height, and we see it for what it is, a vast field of carved rocks, rolling over a hill. It's a cemetery for dead humans. The bunny goes crazy thumping: terrified, honking and grunting, his ears laid back. I go to his side, to find out what is wrong. He is sniffing the air, his ears wide and apart. It smells of death, and a dripping pile of bird shit laced with bone shards confirms the worst. Owls.

He fears the owls. I try to show him he shouldn't be afraid of the owls; though, I too am wary of the aerial predators, but I don't tell him. He fears owls more than the infected, and he believes I should, too. Rabbits may not be able to remember their *name*, but they are hardwired to be on the lookout for anything wanting to eat them. It's no secret wild rabbits and their ilk were the animals my breed of dog were crossbred and designed to kill. Cats, too, have a fondness for rabbit meat. But we are civilized and have *names*. Animals with *names* do not eat each other. Owls on the other hand, well, they top the list of beasts not giving a crap about *names*, or anything human, we've carried over. This includes, but is not limited to, *sitting*, *staying*, or *looking*. Unlike the brain worm infected, owls killed to feed a natural life; they too fought for survival. They are no different than us, making them more dangerous than the infected.

One of the others alerts us; something is near. I scan the sky, knowing I wouldn't see the owl before it struck, if it did. They were silent killers. No, something else, something putrid, but not infected, took this path. I follow the scent, being careful to watch for any sign something from above might be amiss. I make my way through the grass to our growling compatriot, who won't move forward out of fear. I'm cautious, watching the skies with one eye. In doing so I almost tripped on the dead thing's hairless tail. There, lying prone against a headstone, we found a giant, dead rat.

The body still radiates some heat, but it wasn't breathing. Gashes, long and fresh, were cut into its back. It was evident this thing was the victim of an owl attack. But where were the owls? I gaze up at the black sky again. I sneeze and sniff at the dead thing. It has taken ugly to a new level of fright. Despite its horribleness, it didn't smell of brain worms, and none were wiggling about in its wounds.

My rumbling belly reminded me there's one thing we can do. This corpse isn't infected, at least we can eat it before it gets stiff. It's dinner time, and I call the others over and hope I'm not alerting any owls. The pack circles over, including the bunny, who stays back and thumps. He doesn't like this one bit. Something isn't right. The bunny honks. He's been a pain in the ass since we left the burrow, but I still listen to him. Even so, I'm fed up with his constant paranoia. He warns us, thumping to signal it's not dead. It's about all I can take. I turn my head and look at him, raising an inquisitive eyebrow and ear, then I snap a growl. He lays his ears back and crouches into a fearful ball of fur. My mate goes to his side and consoles her friend. She gives me the same look in return. I yawn and sneeze, irritated by this bunny drama. I tap the dead thing's belly with my paw. Nothing. The giant, dead rat still doesn't move. I drop my *ball*, reach forward and bite it.

No warning is given, no sign I'd executed a bad idea. Nothing to alert me the body would be anything other than I thought it to be: a giant, dead rat. Nothing, until a loud hiss erupted from the corpse, almost a scream, confirming the bunny's suspicions. I jump back, as do the rest of us. The dead thing springs to life, spitting and snarling at us. Coarse hair standing on end, swatting at us with hand-like claws. It growls back with ferocity I'd never seen in a rat before. Now I see it in the full moon light, I realize the bunny was justified, once again, in his paranoia. This wasn't a rat, after all. I bit a pissed-off opossum playing dead, a multitasking feat they excelled at, as being pissed off defined their nature, all the time. I think I'd be pissed off, too, if I resembled a giant, hideous rat.

Opossums are hearty and somewhat resistant to many pathogens. As a result, they also tend not to be susceptible to the brain worms, much like birds. Or, simply put, they are so ugly the brain worms were afraid of them, whereas birds were straight up immune. Possums are cowardly by nature, and a good alpha dog like me can dominate the creature with ease. I growl at it, showing my teeth, letting it know I'm not messing around. It hisses, again, in return.

The rest of us soon surround the creature, some growling under their breath. Then it stops, looks up, and plays dead again. It's plain to see the critter is more fearful of any owl than of a pack of dogs. We all look up, in unison, following the possum's lead, but see nothing. After a moment or two of surety, the possum again goes on the move, beckoning us to join in suit. I snatch my *ball* back up and give a garbled command to the others. We will follow the possum.

·

The cemetery is a maze, a near endless field of grass and stone monuments. The perfect killing field for an aerial predator. We move, silent as possible and as slow as our guide, through the grounds. We reach a small grove of trees, and the grasses become shorter and easier to maneuver through. I can see the human house in the distance, beckoning. We're on the right path. One of us walking near the possum marks a tree. The moonlight shines through the branches, revealing a mausoleum on the other side of the small grove. The exit should be near here, I think. Something smells wrong, dead and rotted. It leaves a bad taste in my mouth.

Something crashes to the ground with a wet thud, rustling the tall grass. A familiar odor catches my attention, and I go over to the spot. It smells infected and ... I stop in my tracks. Before me is the mangled and half eaten body of a skunk. I see brain worms writhing about the wounds. Could it be the skunk from the other side of the *highway*? I see the animal's rear end and the gaping hole the infected kits had crawled from, erasing any doubt of its origins.

Before I can bark a warning to the pack, the one who marked the tree starts making his way out of the trees. The possum drops to the ground, not moving, once again playing dead.

But why? The dog doesn't stop, but the rest of us do as a shadow flies in front of the moon. The bunny lays flat and disappears into the grass, shaking and terrified. An owl is overhead.

It strikes without a sound, grabbing the dog by its hind end. The canine squeals in pain, the cry echoing through the cemetery grounds. He struggles to get free, thrashing in the steel grip of the bird's talons. We can do nothing to help. All we can do is hide. High in the air, the owl drops the dog. He plummets to the ground, landing head first on a block of granite. His neck snaps on impact. The owl swoops back down on his kill and starts feeding. There is no further sound from our former companion, except for the ripping and tearing of his flesh.

Owls hunt in packs, and where there is one, there are more. As if on cue, a large owl lands on the possum's back. The raptor pecks once at the marsupial's open wound, then hops up onto a nearby headstone. The possum stirs and crawls behind the bird's perch. The lead owl stares at me and blinks. The bird cares little about a showy visual display of dominance. It knows it has dinner in its clutches. Or so it would like to think.

I look about and see bones scattered in the low grasses. It's all too obvious the possum led us into a trap. Desiccated corpses litter the grounds here. I bark and urge the pack to follow me as fast as they can run through the grass, past the mausoleum and on to our distant sanctuary.

Another owl swoops at my mate, missing her shoulder by hair. I experience a close call, as well, when one of the raptors pounces at me from above. I dodge away, and the bird flies face first into a gravestone and is stunned. One of the others in the pack wastes no time assaulting the downed bird. The full force of his barreled chest slams into the raptor. Its wings break with an audible snap. The dog growls and bares his fangs, there is no other warning he gives, before he strikes, snapping the bird's head off with one bite. Blood shoots out from the gaping wound, covering feathers and fur in gore without prejudice. He rears his head back to strike again and stops, his ears alert. His head snaps back. He hears something from behind. The large alpha owl attacks, its talons burying into the dog's shoulder.

The dog cries out and rolls into a headstone,

forcing the owl to release it. The dog scampers away, blood pouring down his forelimb, as the owl takes flight. He recovers and shakes his head, like something else is bothering him. Then I hear it, too, a familiar sour tone. It makes me sick to my stomach, not because of the sound, but because I know what it beckons. Brain worm-infected bats.

A cloud of bats obscures the moon. We watch from the ground as an aerial battle commences. The owls waste no time in changing the focus of their attention to the incoming threat. They fly into formation and attack the infected swarm. With precision and determination, the owls strike at the bats, avian talons ripping infected mammals in half one at a time. The carnage is spectacular, and in moments we find it's raining blood, body parts, and worms. The opossum, still playing dead, is covered in viscera.

Not all the owls are victorious in their effort, though. Much like the manner in which they devoured our friend the cat, their numbers allow the bats to swarm upon isolated owls in flight, smothering them. One at a time, they take raptors out of the battle. The infected things rip the feathers and flesh from their victims and scatter, still in flight, as the birds' remains fall to the ground with clunky thuds. There are no winners in this battle.

I look about and see my mate at my side. I can't see or even smell the rabbit. I fear for his well-being, but then I remember how crafty he is, and my concerns are set aside. The rest of the pack is huddled close to one another, a dog phalanx fending off errant bats coming too close. For the time being we no longer worry about the owls, they are too busy defending their turf from the invaders.

We jet past the mausoleum and discover a small wooded grove between the cemetery and the human house. I give my *ball* to my mate and send her off with the pack. They run ahead with due diligence to the wooded lot and the sanctuary of the building beyond. Once they make it to the trees and bushes, I turn back to find bunny. I won't leave him behind.

I dash about looking for our floppy-eared friend. I don't need to look long. Near the mausoleum I find the alpha owl circling about in a tight pattern. I catch an amber glare of bunny's eyes in the moonlight and know straightaway what the owl is hunting. I run forward to my friend's aid, attempting to distract the owl long enough for bunny to hop to relative safety. It's a brilliant plan, until the opossum shows up, blocking my path, hissing and snarling.

We size one another up for an inevitable lightweight showdown, dog versus opossum, with lives at stake for the gate. The opossum doesn't look right. It's hunched over and moving with a strange gait. The marsupial is covered in gore, creating a viscus scene, making the beast uglier than its cruel genetics ever intended. The possum smells of infection, and I see where the brain worms worked their way in, through the owl's claw wounds on its back. It snaps its jaws at me, saliva ridden with brain worms splashing into the air. I return the threat, biting at the air, and the cautious standoff continues.

Then it makes its move, lurching forward, the brain worms in complete control of its body. I'm ready for the strike and dodge to the side. I'm counting on its natural lethargy to work in my favor. The creature is confused for a moment, just long enough to allow me an opening. I rear back and lunge at the opossum from behind, and get body checked by a dive-bombing alpha owl. It knocks the air out of my lungs. The big owl doesn't know the opossum isn't the opossum anymore. I try to warn the owl as the bird lands on its perch at the possum's shoulder. It doesn't listen. The infected animal twists around and bites the owl's leg. The bird's wings spread out to their full length, almost six feet across. With a mighty swoop the raptor shoots straight up, but its leg remains in the possum's mouth. Blood sprays us from the owl's wound as the bird flies to the top of the mausoleum and toward their nests.

I take advantage of the situation and make my way to bunny. He's lying flat, digging in, snorting and honking in fear when I find him. I urge him on, to run. He does, hopping high into the air in a leaping bound.

The opossum snaps and growls and hisses at the wounded owl, scratching at the mausoleum walls, ripping out its claws in the process. The bunny catches the infected marsupial's attention as he runs by at Mach-rabbit speed. The opossum has no chance in hell of catching bunny, but I bark and distract it anyway. The opossum turns to me and charges.

A four-legged hissing visage of hell pounces from the tall grass, landing on the opossum. It's skinless, with small patches of black fur spotted about its body. If it ever possessed a tail, I couldn't tell. The skinned thing sinks its fangs into the neck of the opossum, and they roll over. The thing's hind legs dig into the possum's belly, eviscerating the infected creature with an expulsion of intestines and gore. It hisses and growls. I recognize its familiar timbre. I look into its eyes. My heart jumps. It's kitty? But how? I saw the bats kill her.

The *thing-that-used-to-be-kitty* stands up from the dead opossum, viscous ichor dripping off its gore-slicked body. It takes a few steps forward, wobbling as it does so.

Oh, kitty, what happened to you, my friend? The bats, they chewed off her tail, most of her skin, but she somehow dug deep and found the desire, the urge, to survive.

Kitty drops into the grass in front of me, her breathing shallow, and I see she is dying.

There is a patch of kitty's fur left near her neck. I groom her for comfort, best as I can, licking the spot. She purrs, then a final breath escapes from her body. My friend dies at my feet.

The alpha owl hoots from the nest, calling the pack from the battle. For the second time tonight, I can't stop to mourn my fallen friend. However, I won't let the owls eat her. I push her into the rut bunny dug out, as it's deep enough to at least hide her from becoming lunch. As I kick the dirt back on, I see the other owls arriving at the perch on the building. I take a moment to piss on the dead possum, a good drenching spray. It connects with the brain worms and soon a cloud of disintegrating brain worms has created a fog of cover. I run off as fast as my feet will take me to the wooded lot below, hidden in the mist, before the owls notice I'm gone.

A cloud of bats obscures the moon. We watch from the ground as an aerial battle commences.

Next to a cemetery lies a church, a large rectory and greenhouse. The grasses surrounding it have grown high, but the house and surrounding property are otherwise untouched by the consequences of the plague. Even in times of desperation, holy places are typically left unmolested. Nobody wants to piss off the Almighty when the end of the world comes around.

The moon, now hanging high in the night sky looks to be supported by the church's tall steeple. The cross at its peak casts a shadowy silhouette against the lunar background. The moon itself reflects back from the windows on the third floor of the rectory house.

Tacked to the wooden doors of the sanctuary is a notice. Printed in red, bold letters across the front of the placard read:

SANCTUARY CLOSED

Once capable of stopping a human in their tracks, dogs and rabbits do not know the meaning of the symbols, the words, and thus are immune to their pseudo-magical powers. They do not even understand the meaning of a holy place or holy ground. All they know is the shelter offered by the still standing human structures. To them, the sanctuary is open, not closed. But they must first solve the riddle of how to enter their Elysium...

•

A house rises from the tall grass, an imposing, impenetrable tower stands before us. The windows are dark, but the building appears to be intact. We discovered asylum, at last. Or was it there to taunt us? I wished the kitty-cat were here, part of me praying she would rise from the dead, yet again, showing us the way in. Poor kitty-cat, I miss her already and know she will never come back again. Old and wise, she would know what to do. She would be cautious. She would consider all options. I do the same.

I tell the pack to *stay*. I circle the perimeter, running around the house. All the doors are shut. The windows closed with the glass still intact. Our entrance is forbidden. *Where could she have found entry? Did she climb?* I look up, but disregard the thought. She wouldn't bring us here if we would be forced to climb, our claws are not made for scaling walls. The way in must be on the ground level. I return to the pack and enlist their aid. My mate is exhausted from the journey. She lays down, the rabbit by her side. He stays with her as the rest of us weave in and about the hedges and fencing around the house and garage.

It doesn't take long to find a broken window pane. One of our packmates calls for me when he discovers it. I go to him, checking the area for any dangers. Hidden behind a wind-blown plastic bag, it leads into the basement. I find no infected scat, no dead bodies, nothing to harm us, no scents to concern. I go to my mate and let her know we've found it. She is relieved. I take my *ball* from her, and we join the pack, which is now awaiting my orders.

We make our way into the house's basement, careful not to cut ourselves on the broken glass. Under the window is a large sink. Jumping in is no issue and getting out is a simple leap. For the dogs, even my mate, it's a piece of cake. The rabbit makes it through the window and into the tub without a problem, too. Getting out is another story for him. His fur-covered feet, unable to get friction on the basin's surface, keep slipping and sliding. He's stuck. He can't even jump. He honks in fear and thumps, creating a thundering boom like a human firing a gun. It shakes the feet of the sink and gives me an idea. I put my *ball* down and pull on the leg of the sink. It wobbles and tips but corrects itself. The bunny is throwing off balance. The pack sees this and joins me in moving the legs. The sink topples over, creating a huge racket, and the bunny hops out. He runs around me in a quick circle, nudges my back leg and jumps, clicking his hind legs in the air. He is grateful.

We find the stairs going up to the main floor of

the house. To my relief, the cellar door is open, and leads into the kitchen. There is a dining room, with tables, rugs, and chairs. Everything you would find in a human home. Well, everything except a human, to my disappointment. This place is much like the home I lived in with my humans. It makes me miss them.

In the larger living area, there are recliners and sofas. My mate finds a blanket on the sofa, pulls it off and makes a nest in a corner. The humans who once lived here placed a basket, big enough for my mate and the coming puppies, there. It's almost as if they'd anticipated this. The humans here were dead, like all the others attacked by the brain worms. Humans were the lucky ones. Brain worms didn't drive humans mad, turning them into flesh-eating freaks. No, it killed them within hours of contracting the parasite, just like it did to the *Boy* and would've done to the *Momma* and the *Daddy* if they hadn't died first.

I jump on the counter by the sink. I nudge the spigot with my nose. It turns, and to my joy, water runs from the tap. Water will not be an issue. Food is the next problem to remedy. I send out the pack in tandems, watching each other's backs, to explore the remainder of the house. I stay with my mate and the rabbit. The rabbit hasn't been having a good go of things. He keeps slipping on the flooring. Lucky for us, the humans placed rugs about the place, which he uses like stepping stones to get around. He honks and grumbles, asking me why we were forced to leave the burrow. My mate reminds him of the squirrel attack. Rabbits often forget when they ate their last meal; this is common. His memory refreshed, the bunny lays down and chews on the carpet, relieving his stress.

I go to nest by my mate and rest, and realize I left my *ball* in the basement. I sneeze, annoyed, and make my way back into the cellar. I find my *ball*, right where I left it. I snatch it up and notice something is off. The broken window. It's bigger. And there is hair and flesh on the frame. I couldn't recall if we left it in this condition. I sniff around the toppled sink. Something foul and infected, I'm sure this scent wasn't here before. *This can't be good,* I think.

I turn and run back up the stairs. I stop and push the door closed. It latches, and I dash into the living room expecting the worst. Everything is fine. The rabbit is hiding under the table grazing on the rug, and my mate is sleeping. She opens an eye to verify it's me there. Though nothing seems amiss, I remain vigilant. I hear a commotion from the dining room. Fearing the worst, I drop my *ball* and warn those coming. To my relief, it's some of us, those returning from the garage. They are dragging a heavy bag with a picture of a large dog on it. They found food. Soon after, the others come from the upstairs. It's all clear. The sun rises, shining through the windows.

I warn all of us to be aware of the infected because they can see better during the day. My mate is worried, which causes the rabbit to become agitated, a snowball effect I'd rather avoid. I run damage control and assure them the rest of us have it under control. We lay about the room, being careful to pick spots covering all entrances. My *ball* is the only solace I have for escape in this crazy world. I chew it. Sleep comes, albeit fretful and with little rest for any of us. To my relief, the morning goes by without any fanfare or disturbance from the infected. We have food, water, shelter in relative comfort. All of us but our floppy-eared friend.

The rabbit finds long-dead plants setting on a table near the sofa to tip over and graze upon, spilling dirt everywhere and making a general mess of things. Humans wouldn't like this and neither do I. A *bad dog* would be sent to their *crate* if they did. But the bunny is a bunny, and that's how bucks do things, I've learned. They don't know any better. It becomes obvious, we must find something other than dog food for the bunny to eat.

We need a way to get in and out, for us to go *outside*. We wouldn't *potty* deep in the burrow, why *potty* in a human house? It was another infraction worthy of sending you to the *crate* if humans had a say in the matter. The problem at hand though is finding an easy exit, one not capable of compromising our safety. I look about, near the front door which leads to a porch. It's made of wood, which is good for us. If we dig at the door hard enough, we can make a way in and out.

We take turns, scratching and chewing and being careful not to get splinters. There are no more *vets* to see if we get hurt, and a splinter in the paw or mouth can kill you. After becoming irritated with our racket digging at the door, bunny decides to help. His teeth are iron sharp wood destroying instruments. In no time he becomes our superhero, tearing out large chunks of wood from the door and surrounding frame. After a bit we break through, and soon after there is an opening big enough for us to pass.

We rest again. I curl up next to my mate. Things are starting to look up. Yet, despite all the good favor working out for us, I'm not content; in fact, I'm unsettled. I wish kitty were here to see all this. I wish the other dogs we lost on our way to this sanctuary were here. And wishing like this always ends in disappointment. *Would it today?* I'm not sure. I'm hoping for the best, because as soon as one crisis is averted by our group another rears its head. Thus far we've made it through them all with limited casualties.

•

The little dog finally sleeps. Nested to his mate, safe inside a human dwelling, he can rest easy, but doesn't. He kicks and whines, a sharp and penetrating whelp raises the ears of the other pack members laying about the room. His rest is fretful as dark and horrifying dreams come to life. Being a dog, he does not understand this is his mind processing the day's events, all of his worries, fears, and experiences are separated and cataloged. Through this mental operation, nightmares invade his state of unconsciousness. His legs twitch, and his heartbeat increases.

•

My mate whimpers, letting me know it's time. The puppies are ready to be born. I nudge her along, guiding her to the box the *Momma* prepared especially for this event. Filled with soft fleece blankets, my mate lifts her front paws and tries to hop in, but her belly, full with puppies, holds her back. She can't jump over the lid into the creche.

Everyone is here; it's like nothing happened, and I've dreamed this whole nightmare of brain worms. The *Boy* plays with the bunny, dropping a paper towel roll in front of him. The rabbit, in turn, picks up the tube with his teeth and throws it to the side. Kitty is here, sitting on the stoop of the staircase, her tail swaying to and fro, watching and observing. They're all oblivious to our trouble.

I hear the *Daddy* and the *Momma* talking in the other room. They sound panicked. The words I recognize coming from them are terrifying. *Vet, shots, worms* ... and my mate's *name*. The floor shakes; the *Daddy* storms into the room. Blood covers the top half of his shirt. His neck is ripped open, his head lolling slightly to the side.

Sit, stay! He commands, slurring the words. The *Momma* runs in from behind him and grabs his shoulder, spinning him around and blocking her from my view. She mumbles words I don't recognize and pushes the *Daddy* down to the ground. The top of the *Momma's* head is gone, opened up and hollowed out like a cracked nut. Whatever was supposed to be inside her head was instead dripping over the edges of the exposed bone. I tuck my tail and drop my ears, snarling a warning to the *Daddy* and the *Momma*. The cat runs to her master's side and jumps into her arms.

The bunny screams, sending a shiver through my body. I look to see the *Boy* holding his pet high above his head, grasped in his fist by the hind legs. Brain worms flicker about the *Boy's* eyes and lips, dripping down his chin. I hear the kitty meow and purr. The *Momma* is petting the kitty. Each stroke of her hand removes a patch of fur and skin from the cat's body, leaving red streaks of blood, sinew and muscle.

My mate collapses on her side, her breathing labored. I see the head of the first puppy burst through from between her rear legs. It's a boy pup, and I'm relieved to see there are no brain worms. I'm licking the pup, cleaning off the afterbirth when my mate howls in pain. Something is wrong, her underside is quivering, bubbling. It builds to a boil until at last her belly explodes without warning, spraying the room with brain worms and blood.

The little dog's sleeping anxiety attack reaches a fevered pitch as he kicks, shakes, and whines in place. This wakes the rest of his pack and sends the rabbit into a thumping frenzy. The little dog stretches and lays still, finally, if only for a moment, until he's called by the mother of his puppies.

•

My mate cries out, and I jump up, alert, looking for danger, shaking the lingering memories of the nightmares from my head. There is no risk, the rest of the pack is on watch, but I see my mate's water has broken. It's time for the puppies to come. The whole reason for moving here from the burrow is now happening. She makes her way to the basket of blankets and settles in. I *sit, stay,* and *look,* watching the magic of birth with the bunny by my side. The pack is on the lookout for anything out of the ordinary, inside and outside of the house. Just to be safe.

The puppies come one at a time until there are five of them, all healthy, but all blind and helpless. All vulnerable to brain worms. All without *names*. I'm proud and terrified all at once. *What will become of our puppies, I wonder, in this new world? Will they survive? Will they grow strong and smart like me? How can they live without humans to teach them?* I've got so many questions to which there are no answers, except for the passage of time. I'm glad no nightmares have come true. There's no brain worms to be found, nothing exploding out of her belly, only healthy pups.

I hear one of our packmates calling for aid from the back of the house near the kitchen. I race to his side and discover the basement door, which I closed earlier, ajar and open. The smell of infected rot rises from the cellar. I look around, but there is nothing else amiss. I shake and sneeze, my metal tags jingling against one another, concerned and bothered by this latest development. I look to the other one, who's in the dark as much as I am, not sure what to think of it, either.

The other one of us *sits* and *stays*, watching for anything else out of line in the kitchen. I run back to the living room, my claws tapping on the hardwood floors. I reach the first rug, and notice the tapping of my claws continues. But it shouldn't. I stop. The tapping continues. I look about, twisting my ears for calibration. It's coming from above us? I move my head and point my ears up. No, it's not up, it's to the side of me? I sniff the wall, the clicking becomes more audible, clearer. Whatever it is, it's in the wall.

And it smells dead.

I bark to the pack to join me. They come, all but bunny and my mate, who stay with the puppies. We race into the living room, then up the stairs to the second floor. The stairs twist in a circle and are difficult to maneuver, with small pieces of fabric covering polished wood on each step. A slip on the hardwood caused one of the others to jam their knee and fall down a step, bringing a yelp from the pain as they recovered.

Once upstairs, we find the clicking and rattling in the walls is stronger and louder. We trace it to a bedroom. We sniff around the room. There isn't much to alarm us at first: a bed, a table, and a dresser with a TV. There's a closet covered with a curtain, behind which are shoes and clothes. But a closed door has a musty scent, and my guess is it leads to an attic. And underneath it is the smell of the brain worms. Whatever the intruders are, I'm certain of a couple things. First—they're infected, and second— they're hiding, amassing, up there in the attic.

I bark at the pack to *stay* and *look*, and I make my way back down to the living room. The stairs, again, prove to be problematic, and I almost lose my footing as the twisting stairs throw off my inner ear and sense of balance. I get to the bottom and take a moment to place my center of gravity, and then see everything is okay here.

Bunny is with my mate who is feeding the puppies. She looks up to me, peeking over the edge of the basket, and smiles. It's obvious she's tired and exhausted from giving birth, but she is glowing with the gift of the six healthy lives suckling her. I move closer to the side of the basket and peer in at the beauty of our pups as they nuzzle. They're so innocent, so serene. My heart is filled with joy. I run in a circle, my tail wagging.

The joy is short lived; it's broken by a piercing yelp. I snap my head to the sound to see a dead dog flopping down the stairs. Its neck is ripped open and spouting blood on all nearby surfaces, leaving chaotic streaks of gore as it tumbles down the steps. Bunny honks and thumps. It's a loud crack which scares me more than our dead friend. I drop my *ball* in the basket with my mate and the pups, then shoot the bunny a look to *stay*. Terrified, I make my way up the spiral stairs, one step at a time.

Once I reach the top, the upstairs is a scene straight out of a nightmare. Blood and guts are everywhere. Gore is dripping from the walls and ceiling, puddling on the floor. One of the others, at least half of them, greets me. What's left of them is split apart at the rib cage, its inner organs gone. I'm scared to death. I see more dog parts are scattered about the hall. All of them are dead. *What could do this?*

Then I hear it, a chattering, coming from the bedroom. I make my way down the hall, trying to avoid stepping in a blood puddle. It's not an easy task and paying attention to this almost gets me killed. I look down long enough to decide where to step when a ball of matted fur, covered in pieces of flesh and dripping in viscous, worm-infested fluids, falls on the floor in front of me, blocking my way into the bedroom.

I raise my head to discover it unfolding and standing on its short, hind legs. Blood drips from its extended arms, waving paws with small hands as it growls and snarls, the brain worms controlling its every move. I don't recognize what it is at first, but I note a dark stripe of fur crossing its eyes, and I realize this is an infected, flesh-lusting raccoon. He's three times my size, with powerful jaws capable of snapping one of my legs without hesitation. The lifeless body of the last of the others in the pack is hanging from the raccoon's jaws. It opens its mouth, and the dog's body falls to the floor with a thud, splashing the blood and covering the hardwoods.

My first instincts kick in. I growl and move back from it, to the stairs. If I must fight the creature, it will be on my terms. Whatever I do, I can't let it get down the stairs. The bunny is of no help against this;

I must stop it, or all is lost. I bark and growl, holding the coon's attention. Then I hear the rabbit scream.

Bunny never screams.

It's a high, ear-piercing screech, designed in purpose to freeze your soul. I turn and bolt down the stairwell, careful to watch my footing as I descend, hopping down with two feet and almost slipping more than once in my haste. When I reach the bottom of the stairs, I feel fear and despair. Two more infected raccoons are circling around the rabbit, my mate, and the puppies. They're smaller, walking on all fours. Bunny is trapped with my mate and the pups, and one of his ears is clipped and bleeding. He's got nowhere to run, his feet slipping on the hardwood, unable to get a good enough grip to leap over the infected. His butt is backed up against the basket, keeping him upright. My mate is covering the puppies, growling, trying to scare the coons, but they don't know fear; not anymore.

I take all this in and make my decision. I do not hesitate to start ripping into them. I leap off the bottom step at the one closest to me, my fangs glaring.

I *bite*, I *shake*, I *pull*, and I *tear*, and I *fight*. I show no mercy, I give zero craps for the well-being of what used to be a pair of nice raccoons at one time. At one point not so long ago, they lived a life of pseudo-luxury: sifting through dumpsters, eating day-old bread, and drinking expired milk.

But they're not what they were anymore. Now they are infected with brain worms, and dumpsters and bread are replaced by living flesh.

I duck behind the first one and grab its haunch, hamstringing the thing. It flops around to try and bite me, giving me an opening to lunge forward and bite it in the neck, ripping out a glob of foul-tasting flesh. Blood shoots out of the wound in an arc. The wounded coon flops and kicks, and it brings its hand up to its neck, clawing at it. The blood still finds its way out. It kicks a few more times, then goes limp as the blood pools around it.

Meanwhile, the dead coon's buddy has been snapping at me and biting at the air the entire time, unable to reach me because of his writhing friend. The coon climbs and stumbles over the dead body. I notice the thing is already missing two legs, both on the same side. Gnawed off and healed over, this tragic event happened long before the brain worms came. Regardless, it wasn't an asset to the thing now, making the climb a mistake in the grand scheme of things. I take advantage of the situation, growl and meet the raccoon as it tumbles off the corpse.

My teeth sink into the soft of its belly. The flesh and fur give no resistance to my fangs. I start pulling intestines and organs out, throwing them about the living room covering more of the walls, carpets, and furniture. Guts drip off my snout. I imagine I look as terrifying as the coon. I'm doing what must be done to save the puppies. The infected scavenger dies.

I lower my head and raise my haunches as I bark in its dead face. Maybe the brain worms can hear me; I don't know, and I don't care. I am victorious.

The rabbit screams again, a desperate and alarming screech. I turn my head to see the big raccoon from upstairs reaching down between the rails. It's grabbing bunny by the scruff and lifting him. Bunny is big for a rabbit, and he kicks and thrashes, but the coon doesn't let go. His long-clawed paw has cut into the rabbit's scruff, preventing him from escaping.

I charge up the steps and barrel into the coon. The strength of the blow forces the creature to drop the rabbit. It jerks, to find its arm and hand are now stuck in between the railings. I position myself between the coon and the bottom of the stairs. I see my mate covering up the puppies below, shielding them with her own body. The rabbit runs, he's able to hop. He springs to the door and starts pushing aside the shoes we placed in front of our makeshift exit.

The infected monster tries to bite me, snapping at the air. I catch a glimpse of the brain worms swimming in its eyes, driving the animal mad with blood lust. I'm able to stay out of the reach of its maw until it grabs me with a bony stump, catching me under my collar. The raccoon bites me hard in the shoulder. I yelp and twist out of its grasp, snapping the creature's arm in the process. The bone breaks the skin and it squeals, releasing me, as blood swells from the wounded limb.

I *fight* back. I *bite*, I *scratch*, and I *tear* at the raccoon's hide. I rip out tufts of hair and flesh. I *fight* and *fight* harder than I've ever fought before; my mate and my puppies depend on me defeating this thing.

But the big raccoon is too much for even my will. The creature's good hand slips free from the stairwell, and it slaps me in the side of the head. The blow drives my skull into the steel post going up the center of the circular stairs. I lose my senses for a moment, a bell ringing in my ears as I'm dazed from the blow.

The raccoon wastes no time in picking me up and throwing me down the stairs. I bounce off the first one, hurting the bite on my shoulder. I land on the next step on my neck. I feel a pinch, like a flea bite. I don't feel the rest of the stairs or the floor when I land.

From my vantage point on the floor I can see my mate, and I can see the stairs and the infected raccoon halfway up them. I can see the door and the bunny trying to clear a path for my mate and the pups. I watch the bunny hop out through the hole in the door, wondering why he would desert us. Then the door bursts open.

The infected monster tries to bite me.

ed skies become blue as twilight heralds the dawn of another day. Mornings in this post-plague world are not dissimilar from the nights. The symphony of nocturnal insects segues to the whistles of songbirds. The lights of the moon and stars are enveloped by a single celestial body. A pair of shadows stretch across an empty street block, growing as the sun rises. They belong to a man and a girl.

Humans.

Both are armed, foraging through the remains of civilization. At his side is a young girl, no more than 11 or 12 years old. Healthy and brain worm free, looking for others like them, both human and animal, the survivors move with caution. Anyone immune to the virus, or whatever is causing the brain worms to mutate, is an ally. The infected are dispatched with extreme prejudice.

They are a father and daughter. In spite of the odds against them, these humans are among the few who have endured the plague. The duo has managed to avoid infection and survive a winter in the North Eastern United States. They are outfitted for survival and wearing backpacks. Camouflage patterns adorn their clothing, any separations in clothing are duct taped over, giving them silver arm and leg bands. The girl carries a walking stick made from a fireman's hook and lance. It's a wicked weapon capable of killing any number of infected animals with ease. The man holds an assault rifle. Painted on the barrel are the words "Worm Killer."

On the horizon a church steeple rises above the treetops. The girl points to it, the man nods in acknowledgment. The pair discover a deer trail leading behind the remains of a grocery and a path to cut across the interstate thruway. A small creek borders the land between the interstate and a cemetery. They see not only is the church still standing, the attached rectory house is also unharmed. A small greenhouse sits apart from the main buildings near a now overgrown garden.

Father and daughter move with caution. Shredded bodies of bats litter the burial plots and headstones of the cemetery. The risk of infection is high, but can be avoided by avoiding the worms. They approach the house and steps leading up the porch.

•

"What the hell?" the man screams as he looks down at the injured rabbit scampering through a hole in the base of the door of the house. He checks the door to the house, and finds it to be unlocked. He hopes the rabbit's presence has been a good sign. As soon as the door opens, he knows it wasn't.

The living room resembles a war zone. A pair of

dead, infected raccoons lay on the floor. An all too alive, albeit infected, varmint stands hissing at them from across the living room, halfway up a spiral staircase.

"Get back," he tells the girl and raises his weapon, firing off a burst at the infected coon. Worm Killer roars to life, spitting death at the infected creature. The animal jerks as the rounds impact its body. Then it falls, the body dead, its head still somehow alive, sliding in between the lattice in the railing. It slides in, the monster's jaws still snapping and biting at the air as the brain worms keep it alive, for lack of a better word to call the animation. The man puts the rifle to his shoulder, aims at the head, and blows it into pieces sending raccoon gray matter, blood, and brain worms into the wall behind. Satisfied the raccoon won't rise, brain worms or not, he lowers his barrel and surveys the room.

"What happened here?" the man asks, looking down at the girl. The soft mewing of the puppies becomes a stark contrast to the hissing, infected raccoon. They see the surviving animals, a female Jack Russell terrier and her pups. She looks to have just given birth. The girl sees them, too.

"Look at the puppies and their mother. They're alive. We have to save them, Daddy!"

"We sure will, honey. We'll need all the help we can get," he replies. "They'll be able to fend off the smaller infected animals. But we have to get them their shots, first."

"Yes, we will! This one has a collar," she said, pointing out a dying dog, his neck appearing to be broken, surrounded by the blood, guts, and bodies of eviscerated and dismembered raccoons.

"I see that," her father said. "Poor little guy. Looks like he died fighting, protecting his pups."

"He's not dead! He's still breathing, Daddy," she yells as she kicks the dead coons aside, and then picks up the beaten and battered dog.

"I know," he said, "but look, his neck is broken, and we can't save him. I'm sorry honey. He's not going to make it."

"I know, Daddy, but he shouldn't die alone, like this."

She holds him tight to her chest and flips over the tag hanging from the dog's collar. She scrapes caked dirt off the metal revealing a name underneath the scratches and faded paint. She speaks the name printed on it.

"*Jackie.* Go to sleep, my brave boy," the girl said, holding the little dog and caressing his neck. "It's Okay; your puppies and their momma are safe with us. You did great, so brave. You're the best dog ever! Such a good boy!"

•

The little dog watches, helpless and unable to move as this unfolds. He's fought well on this day, battling against the odds to ensure the survival of his family. The dog's neck has been broken, but his mind still functions, and he is all too aware of what has transpired...

•

It's humans. Not my *Momma* and *Daddy*, but humans all the same. They are *good* humans, to my relief. The *man* has a gun and killed the infected. The danger has passed. The puppies will be given *names* and get the *shots*. They'll be saved! By good humans, humans like our old home! My mate will get a new *name* for her new life and a human girl to sit with. I am overfilled with joy, though I can't feel it. I can't feel anything, truth be told. I sigh, my breath is shallow, and I can't catch it, but I am happy because I know the puppies will have *names*. They will be strong and honorable.

I hear my *name*; the small *girl* human says it. I've not heard it spoken in so long, it brings me comfort and makes me feel content. I realize she's holding me to her bosom. I wish I could feel her touch, but I can't, the fall hurt me too much.

She tells me I am a *good boy*. I know I am, and of this *fight* I am proud. I *bit*, I *pulled*, I *shook*, I gave a *good fight*. Now all I can see are colors, in a spectrum I've never beheld, so full and bright and rich, beckoning me to follow them...

I think I will.

FOR DAD

REMEMBERING DIEGO

D ogs. They're a human's best friend for a reason. And contrary to popular belief, cats are not the original familiar animal of witches. Dogs are. The temples of the three faced Hellenic goddess of witches, Hecate, were the dog shelters of days gone by. Iconography and images of Hecate show her with a dog at her side. As a witch and a bard, my animal companions are my familiars. And yes, they've always been dogs.

What exactly is a familiar to a witch? Well, that depends on what type of familiar we are talking about. You see, there's two kinds of familiars, spiritual and domestic. Spiritual familiars are just that, fairies or ghosts or other little imaginary imps that help a witch make magic. Domestic familiars are much the same, except they're physical beings, and they're a spiritual connection to the wild and nature. They assist you in making magic. For me as a bard, my magic is in the stories I tell. And thus I present the "tail" of the familiar my wife and I have shared for over a decade...

Twelve years ago, my ex informed me our mutual pet, an 18-year-old rat terrier named Doc Holliday, was suffering from dementia... and they had scheduled a euthanasia date. This tore me apart. I'd hand raised Doc, trained him myself. I took him for the last two weeks of his life, and had him live it up with me. During this time I saw his dementia, tearing his little mind apart. It broke my heart, and the day before his procedure, he ate like a king. I gave him his two favorite things. A big cheeseburger and a beer.

A week or so after he passed, I found myself looking at pets for adoption. And one dog kept resurfacing. This little white, wire-haired fellow in a blue bandanna named Diego. He had been abandoned. Dawn and I talked about it, but decided that now maybe wasn't the best time to take another small dog in. We had Wyatt Earp, still, though he was nearly 13 years old at this time.

Instead of adopting, we chose to volunteer at the SPCA. And, of course, the first dog we saw there was Diego, huddled and terrified, shaking on the cold floor of the pen. Dawn got down on her belly, looked him in the eye, and told him that day she would protect him.

We went to the counter and started yelling at them for penning the little guy, and then we filled out the application to adopt him. There was a short list of candidates, and we learned one of them was actually our neighbor! That Monday I got a call from the SPCA that they had approved us, with the condition that Diego be introduced to Wyatt to make sure they could cohabitate. Wyatt ignored Diego at the meeting and Diego did his own thing. The SPCA said that's good, and they'd get back to us. Two days later, we got the call. Dawn was at work, so I reached out to our friend Kim to come and bring me over to get him, which she did.

When Dawn got home, I opened the door and Diego ran out onto the porch. They saw each other and that was it. They had bonded on the spot. Diego became Dawn's shadow and constant companion. It wasn't without some hiccups.

Diego was in rough shape, malnourished, his teeth covered in plaque. He was going to be a challenge to raise and fix up, but we were ready to do it for him. We learned Diego had been abused. He was fearful of brooms, and could NOT take car rides. His anxiety when out in public was great. But he got along fine with Bacchus, our old chinker cat, and even with Fiver, our house bunny. Hell, when we introduced Fiver to Diego, Fiver jumped six feet into the air. Then one night he and Wyatt got into a fight, and Diego bit Wyatt, bad enough for him to need stitches. We wondered if we had done the right thing. I disciplined Diego (with my voice), and it never happened again.

That summer, Diego was licking a hotspot

and Dawn made the mistake of putting her face too close to his. Diego's instinct has always been to nip, and he nipped Dawn in the lip. The bite was brutal, requiring her to get reconstructive surgery. The poor dog was horrified at what he had done. The surgeon could tell it wasn't a deliberate attack, if it had been, the damage would have been more severe. Still, Diego was put on a bite list.

A year later, during a snowstorm, while I was out walking Diego and Wyatt, a neighbor's Rottweiler attacked us. Wyatt was in our backyard, but Diego was leashed with me. Lucius, the Rotty, charged us. I picked Diego up and placed him on my shoulder to get him out of reach. But Lucius jumped and he ripped Diego off my shoulder. I pummeled Lucius until he let go of Diego. Four years before, shortly after we had moved into the house, the same dog had attacked Wyatt. If the bite had been a millimeter to the left, it would have perforated Diego's rectum and he would have had to be put down.

To say Diego and I bonded that night is the understatement of the century. But he was still my wife's dog. We sued Lucius's owners and settled out of court, recouping the emergency surgery fees. I pressed legal charges, but the dog's owners knew the judge, and used Diego's attack on Dawn to justify their dog's actions. They said they were going to re-home Lucius, and remove him from the neighborhood. They did not.

Wyatt had a vestibular attack a month later. Eight months after that, he passed away. Diego became the senior dog in my family that day at just about 5 years old. 3 months later I heard Wyatt barking in the house, and that told me it was time for a new pet. We adopted Rocket that October.

Rocket was the thing Diego needed. They played tug of war with balls and toys. They hunted vermin together. Snuggled together. They became best friends. All was good in our house. We moved twice. Bacchus and Fiver both passed, and we took in a new baby, Midnight, five years ago this June as I write this.

The vet started getting on us to get Diego's teeth fixed. He didn't chew bones, and the plaque built up. The little dog didn't like people fingering at his mouth and as a result, we were hesitant. Then, back in January of 2023, Diego got an abscess and started bleeding out of his nose. We later learned the infection had caused a hole to form between his sinus cavity and mouth. We were mortified.

Surgery was scheduled and in March 2023 Diego's teeth were removed. It was a major, invasive job. Diego was under anesthesia for twice as long as they would have liked. He never fully recovered. The ordeal was rough on him. We were gone for a week of it at AuthorCon, last year and my wife was a wreck, worried about him the entire trip. Then, when we returned, none of his disposable sutures had come out. We took him in and learned the sutures had failed. They had to put him back under again to remove them.

Three weeks later, Diego had a stroke. We rushed him to the vet. Dawn drove and I held him. He passed in my arms as we were pulling into the vet's parking lot. They attempted to revive him. He came back once but then his little body gave up. Now his ashes sit by Dawn's nightstand.

This little dog, our Diego, made such an impact on the life we lived with him, and the lives of those he encountered. He'll never be forgotten, nor will the experiences we had while serving as his caretakers. Mourning Diego has been hard, a day doesn't go by where a lamenting tear is shed by Dawn or I. But it's getting better, and seeing him immortalized in the pages of this book, through Jeff Perdziak's wonderful art, helps. We'd like to think Diego is proud of this legacy he's left behind. I guess we'll find out when Dawn and I inevitably join him on the other side.

Thomas R Clark
November 2024

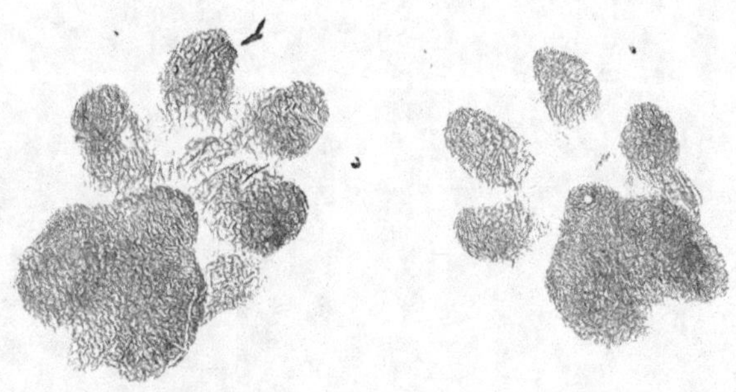

ACKNOWLEDGEMENTS

What you have just read is the result of a family tragedy. We lost our patriarch two years ago as of this seeing print. A void was left behind by my father's passing, and I needed to fill it. This book is the result of that mourning.

On the surface, it's an adventure story starring a dog and his companions. Deep within its narrative, however, is a hidden message, a thank you to my father. Jack Clark loved animals, a trait carried on by my siblings and me, but it's more than that. Thank you, Dad, for doing something innocuous and mundane to most...You gave me a name.

My wife Dawn made this happen with a little help from Dad's spirit. A shout out to my beta readers: Tim, Rich, Rosy, Jennifer, and Bobby for helping keep this real. I can't express the gratitude I feel for Lisa Vasquez at this moment in time—you brought this story to life; you made it something more than I thought it could be—all with your guidance. Fist bump to my line editor, Erin. Thank you for the "threat," Amber, and for saying you'd read this.

This was written listening to The Sword's LOW COUNTRY on repeat. Extra special thanks to Barb

Francisco and her staff of trainers at Petco. in Mattydale, NY for educating me on dog mannerisms.

Finally, this is in honor to the dogs I've had the pleasure of caretaking for during my life. I'm glad I gave you all a name, even if I wasn't always the best human: Charlie, Fonzy, Kingy, Amber, Frodo, Doc Holliday, Dizzy, Wyatt Earp, Diego, Rocket, Midnight, and our new baby, Apple.

ABOUT THE AUTHOR

Thomas R Clark is a two-time Splatterpunk Award Nominee (Best Novella, 2021 for BELLA'S BOYS and Best Short Story, 2022 for FIREFLIES & APPLE PIES). His most recent release, A PRAYER FROM THE DEAD, is available through St. Rooster Books. His journalism and entertainment critiques have appeared in Memento Mori Ink, Rue Morgue, Stranger With Friction, House of Stitched Magazine, This Is Infamous, and miscellaneous internet outlets. Tom lives in Central New York with his wife and their canine companions.